Willow

by Denise Brennan-Nelson
and Rosemarie Brennan
Illustrated by Cyd Moore

In memory of my mom, who loved being an art teacher. —Cyd

For all the nuts on my family tree. —Love, D

For Mom, who had a heart as big as Willow's, and who gave us this story and so much more. —Love, R

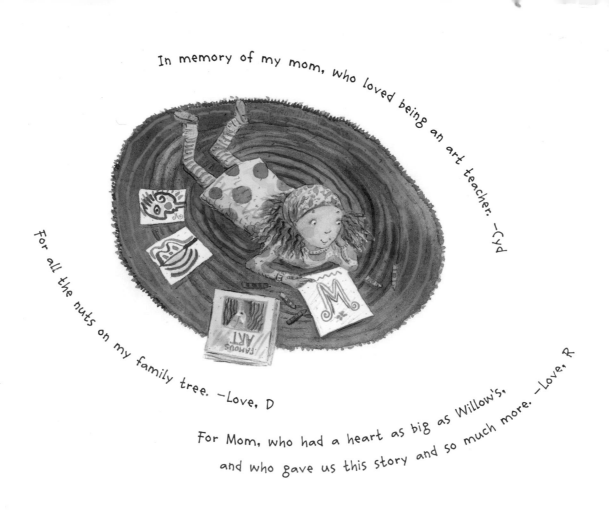

Text Copyright © 2008 Denise Brennan-Nelson and Rosemarie Brennan
Illustration Copyright © 2008 Cyd Moore

Sleeping Bear Press

2395 South Huron Parkway, Suite 200
Ann Arbor, MI 48104
www.sleepingbearpress.com

Printed and bound in the United States.

15 14 13

Library of Congress Cataloging-in-Publication Data

Brennan-Nelson, Denise.
Willow / written by Denise Brennan Nelson and Rosemarie Brennan;
illustrated by Cyd Moore.
p. cm.
Summary: In art class, neatness, conformity, and imitation are
encouraged, but when Willow brings imagination and creativity to her
projects, even straight-laced Miss Hawthorn is influenced.
ISBN 978-1-58536-342-1
[1. Art—Fiction. 2. Painting—Fiction. 3. Imagination—Fiction.]
I. Brennan, Rosemarie. II. Moore, Cyd, ill. III. Title.
PZ7.B75165Wi 2008
[E]—dc22   2007034588

ven on the sunniest days, Miss Hawthorn's art room was cold and dark.

Everything was in its place.

There wasn't a single broken crayon in the bunch.

The students sat in their rows, silent and still, like eggs in a carton.

Except for Willow.

Rosy-cheeked Willow twisted around in her seat to look out the window.

"Face forward, young lady." Miss Hawthorn's icy blue eyes glared at Willow. Willow shivered.

Miss Hawthorn's moods were as dark as her clothing.

One day in September, Miss Hawthorn handed out paper, paintbrushes, and paints. She told her students to make pictures of a tree and hung an example on the board.

All the students painted trees with straight brown trunks and round green tops.

Everyone except Willow.

"Whoever heard of a pink tree?" Miss Hawthorn asked with a frown.

"That's what I saw when I closed my eyes," said Willow.

A few students giggled. Sam snorted, "Pink stinks."

The next week, Willow carried her well-loved art book to school. In it was a picture of a flamingo-pink tree painted by a famous artist.

"Look!" Willow pointed, giving Miss Hawthorn her most magical smile.

Miss Hawthorn glanced at the picture, then turned away with a scowl.

"Horrid little girl," she muttered as Willow skipped off.

In October, Miss Hawthorn passed out paper, paintbrushes, and paints. She told her students to make pictures of an apple tree and hung an example on the board.

All the students painted trees with straight brown trunks, round green tops, and red apples.

Everyone except Willow.

Miss Hawthorn pointed with a long, bony finger. "Look at the mess you've made!"

"And there is no such thing as a blue apple!"

"But that's what I saw when I closed my eyes," said Willow.

Some of the students giggled. Sam laughed especially hard. "Yeah, whoever heard of a blue apple?"

The next week, Willow carried her well-loved art book to school. She showed Miss Hawthorn a picture of a tree with blue apples. Then she reached into her backpack and took out a blue apple. "This is for you," she said, handing it to Miss Hawthorn.

Miss Hawthorn's face turned crimson.

"Horrid little girl," she muttered as Willow skipped off.

It was dark outside when she walked to the cabinet where the art supplies were kept locked away.

Miss Hawthorn filled her arms with paintbrushes, paints, colored pencils, and a sketchpad and carried them to her desk.

She flipped open the sketchpad and stared down at the blank page.

Finally, Miss Hawthorn picked up a colored pencil.

For the first time in her life, Miss Hawthorn doodled.

Outside the wind howled. Trees creaked and strained and broke where they could not bend. Snowflakes swirled upward.

The lights flickered off. Miss Hawthorn sat in the darkness.

When the lights came back on, Miss Hawthorn's fingers found the wet paint and spread it across the page.

The school custodian poked his head into the classroom. He stopped, astonished at what he saw.

Across town, Willow stood at her bedroom
window, peering at the soft, fat snowflakes
through her spyglass.

After awhile, she climbed into bed and fell asleep
wondering if Miss Hawthorn liked her present.

Let
Great
Ideas
Slither
In!

← Imagination Point

Miss H's Stars

← Snake Pit Corner

Josh

Willow

Sam

Behind a graceful willow tree, covered in paint
from head to toe, a woman was painting.

"Grab the paintbrushes! I need your help."

Delighted, the students did as they were asked.

This time, everyone painted just the way they wanted...